Pearl's New Skates

Holly Keller

Greenwillow Books
An Imprint of HarperCollins Publishers

Pearl's New Skates
Copyright © 2005 by Holly Keller
All rights reserved. Manufactured in China
by South China Printing Company Ltd.
www.harperchildrens.com

Watercolors and black line were used to prepare the full-color art.
The text type is Opti Artcraft-Light.

Library of Congress Cataloging-in-Publication Data

Keller, Holly.
Pearl's new skates / by Holly Keller.
  p. cm.
"Greenwillow Books."
Summary: Pearl's birthday skates have a single blade
and learning to use them is harder than she expects.
ISBN 0-06-056280-3 (trade). ISBN 0-06-056281-1 (lib. bdg.)
[1. Ice skating—Fiction. 2. Persistence—Fiction.] I. Title.
PZ7.K28132Pe 2005 [E]—dc22 2004000576

First Edition 10 9 8 7 6 5 4 3 2 1
Greenwillow Books

On her birthday Pearl got a pair of ice skates.

They were white leather, with shiny blades and red tassels.

Pearl loved them.

"They're real ones," Pearl told Grandma on the phone,
"not double runners."
And Grandma made Pearl a red ice-skating skirt.

Pearl imagined herself gliding backward and forward,
like a ballerina on the ice.

She practiced twirling on her toes

and jumping in the air.

And she waited and waited for the weather to be cold enough
to freeze the skating pond.

Finally one day it was.

Mama helped Pearl put on her skates.

Thistle skated over to say hello.

"Come and skate with me," she said.

But Thistle only had double runners

and Pearl didn't want to skate with her.

Pearl's uncle Jack was skating on the pond.

"I see you have new skates, Pearl," he said.

"Would you like me to give you a hand?"

"No thank you," said Pearl. "I don't need any help."

Pearl stepped onto the ice.

It was hard to keep her ankles from wobbling.

"Here I go," she said.

But instead of going forward,

Pearl lost her balance.

She swayed back and forth.

Her arms went around like pinwheels.

Her bottom hit the ice with a thump.

Each time she tried to stand up,

her feet slid out from under her.

Pearl took off her skates.

"I'm ready to go home," she said.

"You don't have to be a ballerina on the ice right away," said Mama.

But Pearl wasn't listening.

The next day Pearl didn't want to go to the pond at all.
She sat in front of the window and watched Thistle
and her other friends pass by with their ice skates.
She tried to read her new library book, but she didn't like it,
and she didn't feel like drawing.

At the end of the afternoon, Uncle Jack stopped in to say hello.

"You didn't come to the pond today, Pearl," he said.

"Didn't you like skating?"

"Not much," said Pearl.

"I like to skate early in the morning," Uncle Jack said,

"before anybody else is there. You might like it then, too."

Pearl said she didn't think she would.

But in the morning Uncle Jack stopped by
just to be sure Pearl hadn't changed her mind.
And Pearl decided to go with him.
"I might not stay very long," she said.
Mama gave her a thermos of hot chocolate
to share with Uncle Jack.

It was a crisp, bright morning. The air was cold but the sun was shining, and there was a little bit of mist rising from the ice. Nobody else was there.

Uncle Jack laced up Pearl's skates. He took her hands
and pulled her out to the center of the pond. He moved away
and Pearl tried to skate toward him.

When Pearl slipped, Uncle Jack pulled her back up.

She tried to move, but she fell again.

"I'm getting cold," Pearl said.

"And hungry and thirsty and tired."

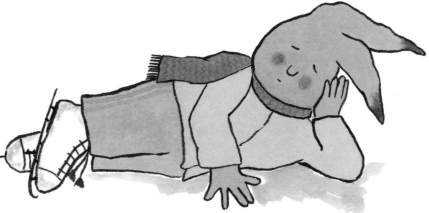

Uncle Jack skated over to pick her up.

"One more time," he said.

"I can't do it," Pearl grumbled.

Uncle Jack skated behind Pearl.

"Look straight ahead," he said, and then he gave her a little push
and let go.

Suddenly Pearl was going forward all by herself.

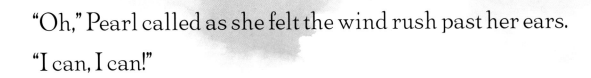

"Oh," Pearl called as she felt the wind rush past her ears.

"I can, I can!"

Pearl and Uncle Jack sat on the bench
and drank their hot chocolate.

"You're going to be a good skater," said Uncle Jack.

When Pearl got home she put on her red skating skirt.

She twirled on her toes

and jumped in the air.

Then she called Thistle.

And the next day they spent the whole afternoon skating together.

JAN   2006